ALEXANDRA GARIBAL is a French children's author and editor. She has written over sixty picture books, novels, and magazine articles, and her titles have been translated for Chinese and Spanish readers. *A Head Full of Birds* is Alexandra's English-language debut. Follow her on Instagram @alexandragaribal.

SIBYLLE DELACROIX is the illustrator of *Tears*, *Prickly Jenny*, *Grains of Sand*, and *Blanche Hates the Night* (all Owlkids). She graduated from the ERG Saint-Luc—School of Graphic Research in Brussels and worked for many years as a graphic designer before becoming a full-time illustrator. Sibylle lives in France. Follow her on Instagram @sibylledelacroix.

VINEET LAL is a literary translator of books from French to English, including *A Perfect Spot* (Eerdmans) and *The Secret Life of Writers* (Weidenfeld & Nicolson). He studied French at Princeton University and the University of Edinburgh. Vineet lives in Scotland. Follow him on Facebook @vineetlaltranslator.

To all the extraordinary Noahs and Nanettes—
both young and old—
whom I met at ABIIF.
— A. G.

First published in the United States in 2022
by Eerdmans Books for Young Readers,
an imprint of Wm. B. Eerdmans Publishing Co., Grand Rapids, Michigan
www.eerdmans.com/youngreaders

31 30 29 28 27 26 25 24 23 22 1 2 3 4 5 6 7 8 9

ISBN 978-0-8028-5596-1 • A catalog record of this book is available from the Library of Congress

Illustrations created with colored pencil

ALEXANDRA GARIBAL • SIBYLLE DELACROIX

TRANSLATED BY VINEET LAL

A Head Full of Birds

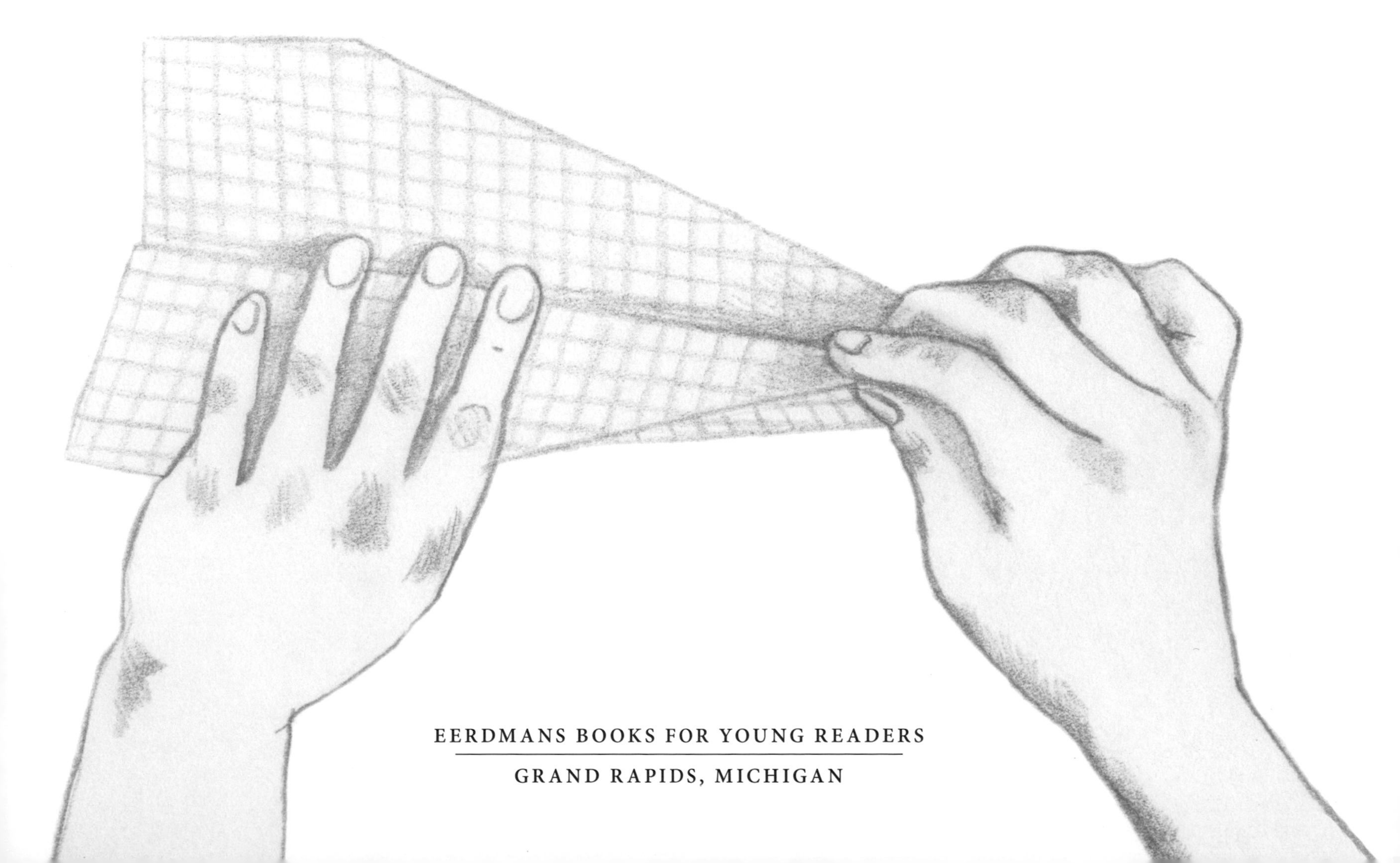

EERDMANS BOOKS FOR YOUNG READERS

GRAND RAPIDS, MICHIGAN

This is Nanette.
A little girl with a head full of birds.

Nanette mixes ham into her fruit yogurt.
She can sit for hours, gazing at a spider's web.
Even though there's no spider.
She rocks back and forth, to and fro,
fluttering her fingers like butterflies.

At school, the kids are nasty and cruel.
"Hey, you! You got a brain in that skull?
Or are you just stupid and dull?"
But Nanette doesn't listen.
She looks down and mutters:
"Skull, dull, seagull."

In Nanette's class, there's a boy named Noah.
One day, during the lesson, he tries flying some paper planes.
Bad luck. One of them lands at the teacher's feet.
Noah is punished. He has to change seats.
"Sit in the front!"

Noah sits beside Nanette. He's annoyed.
He pushes her out of irritation.
Scritch! The sparrow she was drawing is all messed up.
"Oh," whispers Nanette. "He won't fly anymore."
"But birds in drawings don't fly," says Noah, getting angry.
"The drawing doesn't fly, the bird does," says Nanette softly.

After school, Noah sees Nanette
crouching at the edge of the sidewalk.
She's dropping some bright little boats into the gutter.
They fill the stream with color as they float along.
Noah stops, looks at her, and thinks:
That's so pretty.

The next day at recess, the rain is pouring down.
Nanette walks into the middle of the schoolyard.
Then she stands there, not moving, her palms facing the clouds.
Noah's friends point at her:
"She's so stupid! She's so stupid!"

Noah turns his back on them.
And when he sees Nanette taking off her boots
to splash in the water, he rushes out
to bring her back under the shelter.

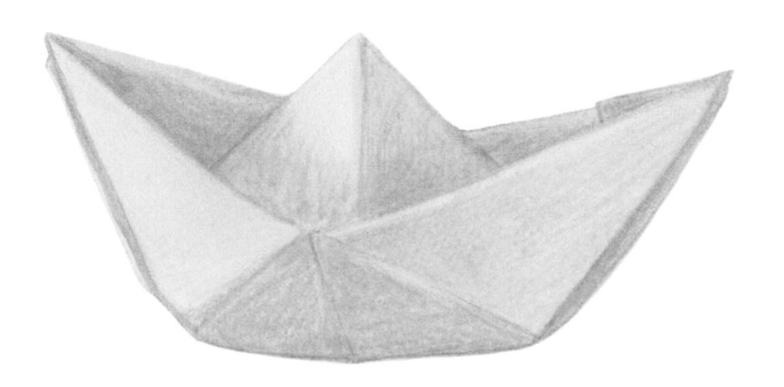

But Nanette doesn't want to move.
"Look," she says.
She fills her boots with the water
streaming off the roof. She hides one under
her raincoat, and hands the other to Noah.
"Quick, let's get back to class!"

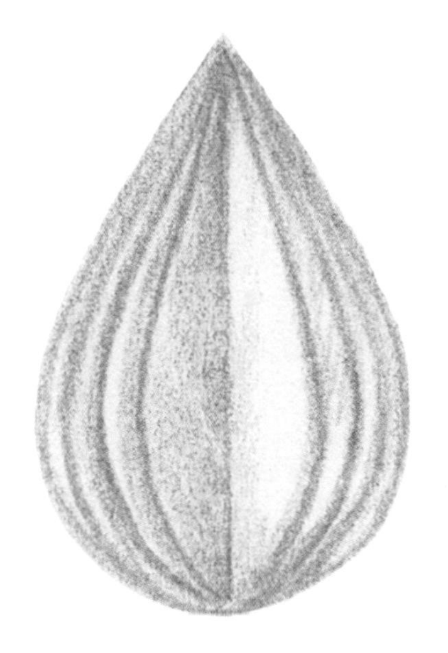

Noah struggles to keep up with Nanette
as she zigzags her way up the stairs.

When Noah gets to the landing, a boy
bumps into him. *Splash!* The boot tips over,
and Noah is completely soaked.
"Watch where you're going!" says Noah angrily.
"Now it's ruined!"

“I’m sorry, Nanette,” says Noah,
leaving the empty boot under his chair.

“Don’t worry,” Nanette says. “One’s enough.” She takes Noah’s hand and slips a tightly folded bit of paper into his palm.

Noah smiles. Then he leans over Nanette's
boot to drop her little gift inside.
The boat twists and twirls,
dancing merrily across the water.
And it's so pretty.

This is Nanette.
And this is Noah.

Nanette is friends with Noah. Noah is friends with Nanette.
Together, they look after the birds that nest in their heads.